'Black Crow's eyes flashed red with fury. His next blow came in an instant. This time Sam was too slow. He felt the cold blade piercing his back. It pushed through his rib cage, his flesh. The sharp point emerged at the front. Streaks of blood covered the black blade.

'Revenge?' He heard Black Crow laugh. 'Is this what you call revenge? Dying like a scared dog, more likely.'

The Last Time I Died
by Fanie Viljoen

Published by Ransom Publishing Ltd.
Unit 7, Brocklands Farm, West Meon, Hampshire
GU32 1JN, UK
www.ransom.co.uk

ISBN   978 178591 139 2
First published in 2016

BREAKOUTS

THE
LAST TIME
I
DIED

Fanie Viljoen

ONE

DYING DAY

The sword struck like a bolt of lightning. It crashed into Sam Carver's blade. The shock sent him reeling. He staggered. The man in the black cloak smiled grimly. 'Had enough, young master Sam?' he asked. His monstrous face twisted.

'No!' cried Sam. The boy seemed older and wiser than others of his age: sixteen. There was a determination in his eyes. With his sword at the ready, Sam straightened up. 'You killed my father, Black Crow. I'll have your blood.'

The crowd watching from a safe distance laughed. Sam

shot a sideward glance at them. A bunch of ugly bastards. Dirty. And scared of Black Crow. Everybody in Old Town was scared of him. He had influence. People who didn't agree with him disappeared. Some say they were beheaded and left for the wolves in the forest. Others were tortured in secret dungeons below the rotten city streets.

I won't be one of them, decided Sam. *This time I'll have my revenge.*

Then a face caught his eye in the crowd. A man in his forties and a friend of his father's. Peter. He seemed to be praying. No, he was murmuring something: 'Stop. Please stop, Sam.'

The swoosh of Black Crow's sword brought Sam back to reality. The blade sliced through his shirt, his skin. A stream of blood came gushing out. The shiny red liquid seemed unreal. The pain was like a red-hot poker. But it sharpened Sam's senses.

He attacked. His dad's silver sword was like a hungry monster, intent on devouring its prey. The crash of metal on metal echoed in the town square.

Clang! Whoosh! Bang!

Sam's injured arm felt weak, but he pushed through the pain. The darkness in Black Crow's eyes spurred him on.

'Argh!' cried Black Crow, as he launched another

attack. The crowd made way as Sam retreated. His back pushed up against a wall.

'No escaping Black Crow now,' yelled somebody in the crowd.

Yeah, right, thought Sam.

Black Crow dashed forward, his sword menacingly above his head. With an almighty blow it came down on Sam.

'You got him!' somebody cried again.

No he hasn't, thought Sam, swooping left. He avoided the lethal blade.

Black Crow's eyes flashed red with fury. His next blow came in an instant. This time Sam was too slow. He felt the cold blade piercing his back. It pushed through his rib cage, his flesh. The sharp point emerged at the front. Streaks of blood covered the black blade.

'Revenge?' He heard Black Crow laugh. 'Is this what you call revenge? Dying like a scared dog, more likely.'

Foul-tasting blood flooded Sam's mouth. It pushed past his tongue, his teeth and spilled out onto the wet cobblestones. Black Crow extracted his sword.

Sam's knees buckled, no longer able to carry his weary body. He fell forward, each breath more painful than the one before. Dying slowly.

Again.

TWO
FATHER

Sam felt something lightly tugging at his body. Then, as if escaping, it raised up, past the bone and skin and flesh. A soul, he guessed.

His soul.

It was light as a morning breeze after a storm. Drifting up … up … up …

He felt free as the Old Town disappeared far below him. Dark clouds enveloped Sam for a second or two. But then a light pierced the clouds, the sudden brightness blinding him.

'Sam,' a voice called out to him. 'Sam.'

It was as if he had awoken from a dream. He was laying on a bed of clean white linen. Everything around him was strange and surreal. It was bathed in a gentle white glow. Even the kind face next to the bed had a soft glow to it.

'*Dad?*'

The man smiled. 'My son.'

'What … what happened?'

'You died, Sam.'

Sam frowned. Faint memories of swords, a man in a black cloak, a crowd of people and blood drifted through his mind. But it was like a dream.

'Did I really die?' He had to ask.

'Yes, son. The sixth time.' His father was cleaning his wounds now. His touch was soft and healing. Sam recoiled when he touched the wound on his chest. But a warm reassuring glow radiated from his father's palms. 'The next life, Sam, will be your last.'

'The *next* life?'

'You're a special boy, Sam. Unlike most people, you've been given seven,' explained his father. 'You've used up six already.'

'Does that mean that I have to go back?'

'Yes, I'm afraid so.'

'But what will I do?'

His father looked at him wisely. 'You've taken it upon yourself to revenge my death. That is your final life's mission.'

'And will I succeed?'

'That is up to you, Sam.'

'I don't want to go back. Let me stay here with you,' he pleaded.

His father smiled. Then he hugged him and kissed his forehead. 'Don't be scared, son. You're already leaving. Your wounds have healed. You'll be fine.' His kind blue eyes touched something deep inside of Sam. It made him want to cry. *It is not possible*, he thought. *He can't leave already.*

'Dad, please!'

He felt his soul drift off again.

'Don't be scared, son.' Those were the words that gave him strength. Those were the words echoing through him as he fell back to earth.

THREE
BURIAL

Like slipping on a shoe, Sam slipped back into his body. It was a strange moment. His senses returned as he felt something hitting him: a heavy thump on his stomach. Then another one on his legs. When a cold and wet mass landed on his face, it shook him awake fully.

'Bloody hell!' he cried, sitting up and spitting out dirt. There was dirt on his face as well.

A loud scream sounded above him. It was a girl.

He stared up in horror at her pale face, framed by strings of black hair. A shovel came down at him, heading for his heart. He rolled away just in time. The blade missed him by inches. It sunk into the wet soil beside him.

'Are you crazy?' he yelled. 'You could've killed me!'

'You're supposed to be dead!' she shouted.

'Well, I'm not, am I?' Only then did he notice the walls of earth all around him. Six feet deep. He stared at the shovel again. 'What's going on here? Were you trying to bury me?'

She wiped the mud from her hands. 'That's what I get paid for, slacker. I bury the dead to make a living.'

'I'm not dead! How many times do I have to tell you?' Sam jumped to his feet.

'You're not my first corpse,' she said. 'I know a body when I see it. Blood everywhere. No breathing. Cold as a rock.' She looked him up and down, as if she still couldn't believe what she was seeing.

He leaned the shovel against the grave wall. Raising his foot, he stepped onto the handle. With small effort, he lifted himself out of the grave.

Now could he see the girl clearly. She was around his age: sixteen, perhaps a year younger. Dressed in worn clothes: a dirty red top and animal-skin coat. Pants stuffed into a pair of black boots caked with mud. In fact, there was mud all over her. Even in her hair and on her pretty face.

Pretty face …

No, Sam, don't you even dare think of her in that way.

'You could've saved me a trip, you know,' she said, crossing her arms. 'I had to push you in that thing all the way from town.' She nodded towards the manky looking wheelbarrow.

'Nobody helped you?' he asked.

'I don't need anybody's help, dead boy. If people help you, they expect something in return.'

He glanced around, taking in their surroundings. They were in an old graveyard. Headstones and statues of angels stood cold and wet around them. There was no sun. Heavy clouds promised more rain later that evening.

'Do you live around here?' asked Sam.

The girl shrugged. He didn't know what that meant.

'My name is Sam,' he said eventually, extending a hand. 'What's yours?'

She stared at him suspiciously, ignoring his hand. 'Claire,' she said after a while. 'I'm Claire.'

Pretty, he thought again.

FOUR

SECRETS

'What are you going to do about the open grave?' asked Sam. 'Leave it? Or fill it back up again?'

Claire shrugged. 'Might as well leave it. People die all the time. Black Crow sees to it. I burn most of the bodies – or what's left of them. There is no ceremony. Just me, them and the fire.'

A chill ran down Sam's spine. 'You *burn* them? But you tried to *bury* me … '

She nodded, pulled her coat tighter around her shoulders.

'Why, Claire?' asked Sam.

She glanced over her shoulder, as if making sure nobody was listening. 'It's a secret.'

'Says who?'

'The man who paid me.'

'You're talking in riddles. Which man? It was *my* burial. I'm sure you can tell me.'

It was getting dark now. Claire lit a torch. The flames danced across her grey eyes.

'There was a man at the fight. He was kind of rich, I reckon. He ... '

'Come on, Claire, tell me,' Sam insisted.

'I ... was doing my work. Pushing your body in the wheelbarrow. The man followed me to the main gate. Outside Old Town he ordered me to stop. "Where are you taking him?" he asked. He seemed like a good man. Kind of handsome for an old guy. "To the Dead Place, to be burned," I answered. He gave me a strange look, then quickly handed me some money. "You need to keep this a secret. Promise me. Don't burn the boy, bury him. He is special." '

'Special ... ' Sam repeated softly.

'Yes.' Claire held the flame up to Sam's face. Then she lowered it to his chest. 'I guess he was right. You had blood all over you after the fight. Your chest, your face, your clothes. There is not a speck of it left now. Is that what makes you special?'

Sam didn't answer. Of course he knew what made him special. Seven lives. One left …

'Look who is secretive now,' said Claire grimly.

'I'm hungry,' said Sam, changing the subject. 'Do you have any of that money left?'

'It's *my* money. Not *yours*.'

'It was *my* death. Not *yours*.'

Claire's stern face changed suddenly. Her lips curled into a smile. Then she let out a roaring laugh.

'What so funny?' asked Sam.

'*You* are, dead boy. Come on, let me buy you something to eat and drink. The town is this way, but I know a shortcut.'

FIVE

SWORD

Darkness closed in around them as they made their way to town. Sam followed Claire up an embankment and down a barely visible footpath. Night animals moved around them as they reached a clump of trees. This had never bothered Sam before, but now …

'Did you hear that?' he whispered.

'Animals,' said Claire. 'Nothing to be afraid of.'

'I know what animals sound like. There was something else.'

'The Angel of Death, perhaps?' she joked. 'He probably noticed you had escaped his wrath.'

'There is no Angel of Death.' Sam would know, he'd died before. But he said nothing of it. 'Listen … ' He grabbed her arm and held her back. 'Voices … '

Claire's eyes widened.

A crack sounded to their left.

Then another twig snapped, closer.

Sam pulled her down behind a fallen tree stump. 'Robbers?' he whispered.

'Perhaps,' answered Claire. There was fear in her eyes. 'We have to get out of here.' Quickly, they straightened up.

'Not so fast,' said a booming voice. A man stepped into their way. Heavy set, a hood covering his face. 'What do we have here?' He reached out and touched Claire's face.

'Leave her alone,' said Sam.

'You brought your little boyfriend along, missy? What are you kids up to?' The man laughed.

Other people were sniggering behind them too. Sam shot a quick glance at them. Two men, also in hoods. They stepped closer.

Instinctively Sam reached back for his sword. His heart stopped. The sword … it was gone.

'Claire, my sword? Where is it?'

'Black Crow took it after the fight. He said it belonged to him now. He earned it.'

Sam's body went cold. They had to get out of there. But without his sword, he felt lost. It was his dad's sword and he'd lost it.

'What do you want from us?' Sam asked the men. His voice was trembling.

'Money, of course. Hand it over.'

'No!' said Claire. 'We ... we haven't got any.'

'She's lying,' said one of the robbers behind them. 'We don't care for liars. Lying breaks the trust, you know. And broken trust makes us ... edgy.'

They all laughed.

Sam's mind was racing.

Suddenly one of the men reached out. He got hold of Claire.

'No!' cried Sam.

The men pushed him aside. He darted back, grabbing one of them by the throat. Earlier he had seen a flash of metal beneath the man's cloak. A dagger. Sam reached out for it. His hand around the hilt. The other hand pulling back the man's head. With a quick movement he slit his throat. Blood gushed out. The man fell at Sam's feet.

In the stunned silence Claire got her wits about her. She jammed her fingers in her attacker's eyes. He yelled out in pain. As he reached for his face, Claire set his cloak alight with her torch. Flames enveloped the robber in an instant. He was like a living torch, screaming and cursing as the fire burned into his flesh.

The third robber fled without a word. Sam and Claire only noticed he'd gone when they got their breath back.

Relief washed over them.

They still had their money. The town wasn't far away.

SIX

FEAR ON THE STREETS

It was a relief stepping into Old Town. Sam and Claire were safe for now. But danger lurked in unexpected places. This was a lesson Sam had already learnt.

He lowered his head as they walked past the guards. They were drunk anyway and would not expect him back in Old Town ever again.

The smell of death lingered in the small passageways. Claire knew her way around, as did Sam. But she seemed to know different ways of getting about without raising suspicion.

Sam followed her as she turned into yet another dark

passageway. Then through a hidden tunnel. They emerged in a quiet square. A fountain trickled into a stone basin.

'Stay here. Hide,' said Claire, turning to Sam. 'I'll get us some food. It would be too dangerous for you to come along. Somebody might recognize you.'

Sam nodded. He watched as she made her way across the square to a street leading to a tavern.

He found himself a hiding place behind a set of stairs. Settling in, he heard something rustle under foot. A piece of paper. A pamphlet. Grabbing it, he held it under what little light came from a nearby window.

Beware
Black Crow has eyes and ears everywhere.
Resistance will be punished.
Death to traitors.

Sam read the pamphlet again and again. Threats like these were at the heart of the fear gripping the people of Old Town. He wished they were idle threats, but they weren't.

Closing his eyes for a moment, he drifted off to sleep. Hurried footsteps and a cry awoke him all too soon. He watched as guards dragged a man across the square. The man struggled free. But as he tried to escape, a flying dagger hit him in the back. He stumbled and crashed to the floor. The guards grabbed him by the legs. They dragged him away. Later, a dark trail of blood was the only evidence left of the horrific incident.

Sam watched in silence. He wished he could've helped the man. But he had his own life to worry about now.

'Hi, dead boy!'

Claire's sudden voice startled Sam. 'What's wrong with you?' he asked.

'Were you scared?'

'Yes … No … '

She grinned. 'Can't seem to make up your mind.' She threw something at him. It was a scrap of clothing. 'I found you a cape. It will help you move about without people recognizing you.'

'Thanks. I owe you one.'

'More than one. But who's counting?' Claire sat down next to him. She stuffed a handkerchief with some bread and cheese into his hands.

'The guards came by,' said Sam. 'There was a man with them. He tried to escape.'

'And did he?'

'No.' Sam pointed to the trail of blood.

'Did they kill him?'

'I don't know. He seemed quiet after they pulled the dagger from his back.'

They ate in silence, occasionally taking a sip from Claire's canteen. Watered-down cider.

'You also had a blade in your back,' said Claire after a while. She wiped her mouth with her sleeve.

'I know,' said Sam softly. 'It won't happen again. This time around *I'll* do the killing.'

'You need help?'

Sam shook his head. 'Somebody once told me that if people help you, they expect something in return.'

Claire sniggered. 'Must have been a very wise woman who said that.'

SEVEN

HATCHED PLANS

Fatigue set in. Sam couldn't keep his eyes open any longer. He made himself comfortable against the wall.

His dreams were wild. Disturbing. Dark. When he awoke the next day, Claire was leaning against him. Her head on his shoulder.

Her hair was in tangles and caked with mud. But she had a sweet smell to her. *Do all girls smell this way?* wondered Sam. He had never been this close to a girl before.

He probably shouldn't have, but he touched Claire's face. Soft skin.

Her eyelids flickered open.

'What are you doing?'

'Um, nothing.' He jumped to his feet and pretended to stretch. He even yawned a few times. 'I'm hungry. Is there any bread left?'

'No, you ate it all, remember.'

'We should get some more,' said Sam.

'No, *you* should get some more, dead boy.'

'I don't have any money.'

'Pity. Then you won't eat.'

'Oh, you're such a girl,' he said mockingly.

She smiled at him. Shook her head. And brought out the small loaf of bread she'd been hiding. Sam tore it in two. He handed her the biggest piece. She exchanged it for the smaller one. 'Wouldn't want you to die again, would we?' she said.

His heart skipped a beat. *What was she doing to him?*

'I've been thinking,' said Sam later, as he wiped the last breadcrumbs from his mouth. 'I need to hatch a plan. I've got to get rid of Black Crow.'

'You mean *kill* him?' whispered Claire. They were still in Old Town. Somebody might be listening.

Black Crow has eyes and ears everywhere.

Sam nodded. 'This time, I have to be strong. I've got

to get close to him. Catch him off-guard.' Sam raised his head. His eyes moved across the tiled roofs of Old Town. On the hill in the distance stood the black castle. 'If I can get into the castle unnoticed ... '

' ... then you could kill him in his bed,' whispered Claire.

Sam nodded. 'Exactly.'

'I might know a way in,' she said conspiringly.

'How?'

She smiled. 'This town is full of secret passageways. And secret tunnels.'

'And you know all of them?'

She winked at him. 'Not all. Only the important ones.'

Sam wanted to hug her. But he couldn't. He shouldn't. 'Wonderful,' he said instead. 'But there is only one problem. An outstanding matter. I need another sword.'

'A sword?' asked Claire. 'Oh, you're *such* a boy.'

EIGHT

EVASION

Clouds were already forming above Old Town. *There would be no sunlight today either,* thought Sam.

'Move your bones,' said Claire. She was striding ahead through the narrow street.

'Where are we going?' asked Sam.

'You'll know when you get there.'

Sam lowered his head as two men approached. His face was hidden by the hood of the cape. One of the men was a blacksmith. The other a horseman. They didn't recognize him.

The relief washed over Sam. He quickened his stride.

'Wait up, Claire.'

She sighed. Stopped. And waited for him to catch up.

'We haven't got all day.'

Side-by-side they made their way out of Old Town. The road stretched out before them.

They didn't talk much. Sam kept himself busy with his own thoughts. Black Crow's face haunted him. *There will be a final confrontation. Who will live? And who will die?*

Sam had died six times already. The odds were against him. And he didn't have a sword.

'You're awfully quiet,' said Claire. She shot a sideward glance at him.

'I'm thinking.'

'Hard work *that*. Thinking.'

'Are you mocking me?'

'No. I would never. A dead boy like you? Who knows what you've got up your sleeve. You might rob me of my soul when I sleep. Perhaps that is how you manage to stay alive.'

'Perhaps,' answered Sam evasively.

Claire's eyes were still fixed on him. 'How *did* you do it? You were dead, I'm sure.'

'Could we talk about something else?' he asked. She might think he was some kind of freak. Okay, he was. But he didn't want it to be that obvious.

A dead boy coming alive? Six times?

Nobody would believe it.

Ahead of them, the graveyard came into view.

'What are we doing back here?' asked Sam.

'Getting you a sword ... ' said Claire and she smiled.

NINE

KNIGHT

There was an open grave. It was Sam's. The shovel was still inside the hole. Claire bent down and grabbed it by the handle.

Is she going to kill me? And stuff me back in that grave? wondered Sam.

Maybe. He didn't really know Claire all that well.

But as they walked away from the grave, Sam gave a sigh of relief.

'This way,' said Claire. She pointed with the shovel. And headed off to an older part of the graveyard. Marble angels and crosses covered the place.

It was late afternoon. The clouds above Sam and Claire were growing heavier. Darker.

This part of the graveyard was a bit overgrown. Long grass. Old trees. Mangled rose bushes carrying heavy flowers. The place smelled of wet soil. And dead things.

No, not things – *people*.

'This one,' said Claire. She stopped and pointed to a grave.

It was old. A rectangular marble slab. With the statue of a knight laying on top. Patches of wet moss grew in the crannies of his armour. His eyes were closed. His hands around the hilt of a sword.

Sam fell silent. It took a moment to realize why Claire had brought him there. 'Is that the sword you were talking about?' he asked.

'No, stupid,' said Claire. 'That thing is marble. The real sword is inside.'

'Inside where?' Sam frowned.

She didn't mean the grave, did she?

Claire handed him the shovel. She *did* mean it. The sword *was* inside the grave!

'No!' cried Sam. 'I'm not digging up a dead guy.'

'You're digging up a dead guy's sword,' said Claire. 'There is a difference.'

'Still. It is grave robbery, Claire.'

'Then I guess you don't really want a sword after all.'

'I do, but not like this.'

'Why not? He's not using it. The stupid old fart was buried with it. He probably thought there were dragons in the afterworld. Or wars to be fought. Who knows.'

Sam's eyes were fixed on the knight. 'No. I can't do it.'

Claire grabbed the shovel from his hands. 'Okay, then I will. It won't be the first grave I've dug up.'

'You've done this before?' asked Sam.

'Of course. When business is slow. Some people get buried with jewellery and stuff.'

'And you dig them up and steal their jewellery?'

Claire shrugged. 'Don't look so surprised, Sam.' She knelt next to the marble slab. 'Help me get this thing out of the way. I'll do the digging.'

TEN

ROBBERS

Sam felt guilty. He shouldn't have, but he did. He was hanging around, watching while Claire did all the digging.

She worked like a mad woman. Strong. Shovel after shovel full of wet earth flew out of the grave.

Sam inhaled deeply. 'Give me the shovel. I'll do it.'

'No.'

'Come on, Claire. I can't stand here and watch a girl do all the work.' He jumped into the grave beside her.

'Are you doing it just because I'm a girl?' she asked. 'Because you think girls can't do hard manual labour?'

'No. It's … it's not good manners to stand here. And watch you.' He grabbed the shovel from her hands. She tried to pull it away, but he held on tight.

Claire smirked as Sam started digging. It was tougher than it looked.

She got out of the open grave. 'You're holding the shovel wrong. You'll tire easily. Grab it lower with your left hand. That's right.'

Sam couldn't believe he took instructions from her. But Claire was right. It made the digging easier. He felt every muscle in his arms and back working.

He sensed her eyes on him. He couldn't show her that he eventually *did* get tired.

One shovel full of soil after the other landed on the heap outside the grave.

Deeper and deeper he dug.

His breath was now noticeably short.

Then he struck something.

'You got it!' whispered Claire.

She jumped back into the grave. Quickly she helped him clear the casket. Some of the wood had collapsed. The rest too was rotten.

'Are you ready?' she asked Sam.

He nodded.

She broke open the rotten wood.

Above them a flash of lightning suddenly lit up the sky. It sent Sam's heart racing.

Huge drops of rain came down on them. Sam tore his gaze from the sky. And stared down on the pale skull. Dark, empty eye-sockets. The blackened metal armour.

A golden sword lay in the knight's armoured hands.

The metal fingers clanged as Claire removed the heavy weapon.

Suddenly an eerie hiss escaped the mouth of the skull. Something unseen hit Claire in the face.

A glint of red in the skull's eye-sockets.

And another flash of lightning, so hard it rattled the skeleton's bones.

ELEVEN

CURSE

'What just happened?' asked Sam.

Claire had fear in her eyes. She handed Sam the sword.

'I don't know. I must have inhaled something.' She was trembling now.

Sam helped her out of the grave. 'We've got to get away from here.'

Again, lightning flashed. Rain was coming down hard now. Their clothes were soaked.

Stumbling through the darkness, Sam and Claire found their way out of the graveyard.

Claire held on to Sam. Her whole body was trembling now. 'I'm cold,' she whispered.

'I'm cold too,' he said.

'No. It's not the same. I've been cold before, Sam. This is different. I'm freezing, deep down to my bones.'

Sam could sense the fear in her voice. He threw his cape around her shoulders. It probably didn't help. The cape was sopping wet.

'I think … I think I might have been hit by a curse.' Claire started crying.

Sam felt helpless. 'We need to get you some help. I know a healer in Old Town.'

'No, it would be too risky. He might turn you in if he saw you. Black Crow uses people as his eyes and ears.'

'But what if you die, Claire?'

He probably shouldn't have said that.

He could see she feared it too, but she answered bravely.

'I'll be okay.'

The words were scarcely out when she collapsed. He took her in his arms. Rain pelted down on her face, washing the mud away.

'Stay with me, Claire,' he pleaded. 'I'll tell you my secret if you stay with me.' His voice shook. 'I've … I've died before, Claire. Six times. I've got one life left. Only one. I would give it to you gladly, but I can't.'

Her eyes were closed, but she seemed to be breathing still.

Could she hear him? He wasn't sure.

It was a long and tiring walk back to Old Town. But when Sam eventually saw the lights of the city walls, he set Claire down. Making her comfortable as best he could, he said, 'I'm going to leave you here for the moment. I can't carry you into town. It would only cause suspicion. But I'll be back with the healer, Claire. I promise.'

Sam gently kissed her forehead. Her skin was as cold as winter rain.

'Don't die, Claire,' he whispered in her ear. 'Don't die.'

TWELVE

HEALER

Sam's heart pounded as he made his way through Old
Town. At times he had to hide in the shadows as people
came past. Then on again. Until he found the door he
was looking for.

He knocked.

Seconds later the door creaked opened.

'Sam?' said the man before him. His father's friend.
The man he recognized in the crowd during the fight.
Peter. 'You're alive!'

'I need your help, sir,' he said urgently. 'My friend,
Claire … she's dying.'

'But are *you* all right?' Peter touched Sam's face as if to ensure it was really him.

'I'm fine, sir. Please hurry. You have to help her.'

Peter's eyes moved to the sword hilt showing behind Sam's back. But he didn't say anything other than, 'Let me get my medicines.'

Soon they were on their way out of town. The rain had let up now. Sam stared into the flames of his torch as he strode on. His thoughts were with Claire.

Then Peter broke the silence. 'That's not your sword, is it?'

'No, Black Crow has mine. I'm ... I'm borrowing this one.'

'It belonged to a famous knight. The dragon on the hilt was his symbol.'

'Did he slay dragons, sir?'

Peter nodded. 'He was a great man. Like you, Sam.'

'I'm not great. I'm just a teenage boy who wants to revenge his father's death.'

Peter smiled knowingly. 'There is so much more to you, Sam. Do you know your destiny?'

'*Destiny?*' Sam frowned.

'When you were born, a sorceress revealed your destiny to your mother: You would have seven lives.

You'll fight the Dark. But only once you discover the Blade of Dragons will you have a chance of winning.'

Sam let the words sink in. 'And shall I?'

'Win?' Peter thought about the answer a while. 'That would be up to you, Sam.'

The answer didn't give Sam the peace of mind he needed. But they were coming up to the place where he had left Claire, so he brushed it off.

Hurrying ahead, he shouted: 'This way, sir!'

The thought of seeing Claire again made him feel warm inside

Sam smiled. 'Claire!' he called out.

There was no answer. It was strange.

No it isn't, said a voice inside his head. *Dead people don't talk.*

She's not dead, thought Sam.

But soon enough the shock hit him.

'Claire?' He raised the torch to see more clearly. Searching the place where he'd left her. 'Claire … '

Eventually Peter caught up with him. 'Sam, what's wrong? Where is she?'

Sam stood there breathless. 'Gone,' he answered, biting back the tears.

THIRTEEN

BAD NEWS

'I shouldn't have left her,' said Sam. 'Where could she have gone? I told her to stay here.'

'Are you sure this is the spot?' asked Peter.

Sam glanced around. It was dark, but he was sure. 'This is it.' The emotion welled up inside him again.

Peter placed his hand on Sam's shoulders.

Suddenly another voice spoke out of the darkness. 'I know where she is.'

An old woman stepped into the light of the torch. Her face was wrinkled. Her clothes shabby. Her breath reeked of rotting fish.

'Where? Tell us!' said Sam.

'Manners, dear boy.' She stared at him. Did she recognized Sam? He hoped not.

'Please,' he tried again. '*Please* tell us where she went.'

The old woman gave a sly laugh. Then she held out her hand. Palm up.

'I don't have any money,' said Sam desperately.

But Peter dropped a coin in the woman's dirty palm. 'Tell us,' he barked.

The woman glared at Peter. 'The girl … She didn't go, she was taken.'

'Who took her?' asked Sam.

The woman kept quiet.

Peter dropped another coin in her hand.

'Black Crow's men took her,' she continued.

At the mention of his name, Sam felt a chill. 'Do you know where?'

The woman shrugged. Peter dropped another coin in her hand.

'They took her away on horseback. To Black Crow's castle. So they said.'

'You've been a great help,' said Peter. He smiled and gave her another coin. The woman bowed thankfully. Then she shuffled back into the dark.

'Do you think she is telling the truth, sir?' asked Sam.

'Nothing Black Crow does will surprise me,' Peter answered.

Sam inhaled deeply. 'Then I'm going to kill him tonight.'

FOURTEEN

FINAL LIFE

'The last time I died, there was a crowd of people watching,' said Sam. 'Tonight it will only be me and Black Crow. And tonight *I* won't be the one dying.'

Sam and Peter were on their way back to Old Town. It felt like a fire was burning inside Sam.

'Perhaps you should consider it again. Don't rush into things,' said Peter. There was concern in his voice.

Sam was stubborn. 'I can't wait any longer, sir. I need to get to Black Crow's castle. Then I'll have to find a way in. Claire said she knew how to enter without the guards noticing.'

'But she's not here anymore, Sam.'

'Then I'll have to figure it out for myself.' Sam was more determined than ever.

'Or you could ask me,' said Peter.

Sam stopped dead in his tracks. 'You know how to get in?'

Peter nodded. 'I'll accompany you and find Claire. You can take care of Black Crow. It is dangerous. I warn you, Sam. We would have to be careful.'

A determined gleam shone in Sam's eyes. 'I promise I will. I can't waste my final life. Not on Black Crow.'

FIFTEEN

DESTINY

Sam and Peter waited in the dark until Old Town fell silent. In the distance Sam could see the outline of Black Crow's castle. His destiny lay there. In some way it scared him. In another, it spurred him on.

Eventually Peter gave the signal. Sam followed him to a dark alleyway. Removing an iron grate at the end of the alley, they dropped down a manhole. Peter lit his torch again.

Sam took in their surroundings. They were in a tunnel below Old Town. The walls were made of rock and covered in moss. Black water, ankle deep on the floor.

'Your father and I used to play here when we were kids,' said Peter.

Sam smiled.

His father.

Hearing Peter talk about his father made Sam miss him.

He said a silent prayer: *Please help me, Dad. I know you're watching. See me through this ordeal. Give me strength. Give me wisdom.*

Sam followed Peter down the tunnel. The water splashed as they made their way to the castle. At times the tunnel narrowed. They squeezed through, helping each other out. At some point the tunnel floor started to slope upwards. It was slippery underfoot. Holding on to the rocks beside them, they climbed the slope. Then onwards again, quickening their pace to make up for lost time.

Eventually they came to a square room. *A basement*, thought Sam. To the right there was a set of steps leading to a platform. At the end of the platform – a wooden door.

'Is that it? The entrance to the castle?' whispered Sam.

'Yes. Are you ready?' asked Peter.

'Ready as I'll ever be, sir.'

'Let's go.'

The door made a fine creaking noise as they opened it.

Destiny, thought Sam. *This is where my destiny lies.*

SIXTEEN

STEALTH

Taking a deep breath, Sam stepped through the doorway. They were in a narrow passage. Another one crossed ahead of them, bathed in flickering light.

Peter extinguished his torch.

In stealth mode they made their way forward. Making sure all was safe, they turned the corner. Then up a small flight of stairs, always keeping to what little shadow there was.

Sam's heart was already racing.

A guard station came up ahead.

They sneaked closer.

'It is manned,' whispered Sam.

'Hey?' came a sudden loud voice from the small chamber. 'Who goes there?'

Sam felt his blood freeze. He should have kept his mouth shut.

The guard stepped out to investigate. His sword in his hand.

Sam and Peter pressed their bodies up against the wall. Hidden by the shadows.

The guard came past. Inches away.

Sam's breath caught. The guard must have heard it. Instantly he swung towards them. Sam could see the rage in his eyes. But only for a moment.

Quick as a flash Peter stepped forward. Dagger in hand.

The guard dropped to the floor as life left him. His eyes glazed over.

'We have to be more careful,' said Peter. 'Help me drag him to the shadows. And clean up the blood.'

The guard was heavy, but they managed. Using a cloak they found in the guard station, they cleaned up most of the blood. A map of the castle was pinned to the guard station's wall. Sam tore it off. It might come in handy.

Stuffing it in his pocket, he heard a faint cry.

'Help.'

Sam and Peter froze. Listened.

'Help me, please,' cried the voice again.

'Claire!' whispered Sam. 'She's alive.'

He started off in the direction of the voice, but Peter held him back.

'I'll help her,' said Peter. 'You find Black Crow. Stay safe.'

Before Sam knew it, he was all alone in the passageway. Peter headed off to the right.

Sam pulled the map from his pocket. He studied it for a second, then turned towards the flight of stairs on his left. The stairs leading up to the castle's ground floor.

SEVENTEEN
STRIKE

Sam had two close calls as he made his way up to Black Crow's bedroom. He had to be patient. Wait it out in the dark until the guards moved off.

Eventually he reached the bedroom. The map helped him find it.

There was another guard stationed at the bedroom door. It confirmed that Black Crow was inside.

Sam watched the guard from the shadows. He was standing at attention, but every now and again his head dropped. He was tired. Half asleep on his feet. *I could take him*, Sam thought.

Quietly he moved closer, hiding behind a pillar. Waiting for his chance. Waiting for the guard's head to start drooping again.

Then!

Sam stepped closer in a flash. The guard didn't know what had hit him until it was too late. Sam's dagger plunged into his neck. He grabbed the guard around his chest. Gently letting him collapse to the floor.

Stepping over his body, Sam placed his hand on the doorknob.

Black Crow was in the next room. Sleeping.

Father, help me, Sam again prayed. The words were only in his head.

His heart raced fiercely as he turned the door knob.

Silently he stepped inside Black Crow's bedroom, locking the door from the inside.

The fire in the hearth gave off the only light. It cast terrifying shadows across the walls.

Sam reached back for his sword.

Then he crept towards the four-poster bed.

Closer.

Closer.

Revenge: This was why he had come.

He moved around the bed where Black Crow lay sleeping.

Revenge.

Sam's fingers closed even tighter around the sword hilt.

Deep breath.

Raising the sword.

Then he struck.

But something was wrong.

EIGHTEEN
FINAL BATTLE

Feathers flew up around Sam's head. Black Crow wasn't in his bed. He wasn't dead.

'Did you really think you could murder me in my sleep?' hissed a familiar voice from the dark.

Black Crow stepped forward. An evil grin on his face.

'My eyes and ears are everywhere, young master.' He swaggered closer. 'I knew you were on your way as soon as you entered the tunnel. I waited for you. You still haven't learned, have you?' Black Crow sniggered. 'Perhaps you will learn now. One life left ... Am I correct?'

Sam nodded. He was mad at himself. He should've thought this thing out more clearly. But it was too late now.

'So, if I kill you tonight, I will be rid of you … forever … ' Black Crow stared at Sam menacingly.

'But if you don't, I will be rid of *you*. Forever! And I would have my revenge. You killed my father. You kidnapped Claire.'

'Claire, dear sweet Claire … ' Black Crow laughed darkly. 'A grave-digging girl and a feeble father are no reasons to lose your final life over.'

'Maybe not to you. But they matter to me,' said Sam bravely.

'Then prove it!' cried Black Crow. His sword flashed through the air.

Sam stumbled back. Turning, he gained his balance.

He attacked. His Dragon Sword clashed against Black Crow's silver weapon. The sword he stole from Sam. Sam's father's sword.

He wouldn't dare kill me with my father's own sword, would he? wondered Sam.

Another blow, then another.

For a moment it seemed as if Black Crow was tiring, but soon he struck back with all his force.

Sam retreated. Black Crow's sword came at him fast. Deadly.

The point sliced through the skin on Sam's cheek.

Blood poured out.

I'm losing, thought Sam, as the blade whooshed past him again. More blood spilled as the blade pierced his shoulder.

Sam cried out in pain. Leaning forward, he grabbed the wound. Saw the blood on his hands.

'Dying to lose, are you?' heckled Black Crow.

No, I won't, thought Sam. *I won't lose. And I won't die!*

In his mind's eye he saw his father's face. He saw Claire. Beautiful Claire.

It gave him the strength he needed.

With renewed hope he straightened up. 'And now *you're* going to die!' he cried.

His sword flashed through the air. Like an army of soldiers all attacking at once, he drove Black Crow back.

For the first time ever he could see fear in his enemy's eyes.

Their swords clanged as they met.

Shivers of pain ran up Sam's arms. But he kept at it. Fighting, fighting.

Never taking his eyes off Black Crow until the final blow came.

An opening. An unguarded moment.

Seizing the opportunity, Sam drove his sword forward. It pierced Black Crow's chest. Pierced his heart.

Black Crow dropped his sword. Defeated, he fell to his knees. Blood spilled out over his lips. 'You beat me,' he whispered, spitting more blood.

'It was my destiny,' said Sam, driving the sword deeper.

'So it was,' answered Black Crow, collapsing at Sam's feet.

Dying suited him.

NINETEEN

NEW LIGHT

The door crashed open. Three soldiers came rushing into the room. But they stopped when they saw Black Crow's body lifeless on the floor.

Sam picked up his father's sword. Then he extracted the Dragon Sword from Black Crow's chest.

Two swords.

One he'll return to the knight.

The other he'll keep.

'Did you come to arrest me?' Sam asked the soldiers.

One of them stepped forward. But a clear voice from the bedroom door said, 'No! Black Crow's reign has ended. The fear gripping the city has ended. You have Sam Carver to thank for that.'

Sam found Peter's eyes.

Peter smiled at him.

'He would make a great ruler, this youngster,' said Peter. He stepped in between the soldiers.

A warm feeling settled in Sam's chest. 'Do you really think so?' he asked.

'I wouldn't lie, Sam.'

Turning to the soldiers he continued. 'Let everybody know what happened. Tomorrow we'll celebrate our freedom. And we'll welcome our new ruler: Sam Carver.'

Sam frowned. 'Are you sure?'

Peter nodded. 'It's part of your destiny, Sam. I didn't tell you everything, did I?'

'No.'

'It must have slipped my mind,' said Peter, smiling. 'Oh, before I forget anything else – there is a lovely girl waiting for you downstairs.'

'Claire?' asked Sam.

'Could be … '

Rushing down to the lobby, the expectation rose

within Sam. One of the maidens pointed him in the right direction.

He found her lying on a sofa in one of the lounges. Her long hair spread out over a cushion. Some loose strands curled in her neck and across her pale face.

'Claire,' he whispered, gently touching her cheek.

Her eyes fluttered open. 'Sam?'

'I can't believe it's really you, Claire. Are you okay?'

She smiled tiredly. 'I'm getting there.'

He helped her to her feet. 'I'm sorry I left you.'

'Don't apologize, dead boy,' she said. 'You tried. That's all that matters.'

Her smile was weak, but it touched something deep inside of Sam. He had never felt anything like this before. It was like the new light beaming through the castle windows. It raised his spirits, made him feel warm. Made him feel loved.

And, as Claire kissed him for the very first time, it made him feel alive.

Fanie Viljoen is a well-known South African children's author, illustrator and artist. He writes in both Afrikaans and in English and some of his books have been published in both languages.

Fanie has written numerous short stories, radio plays and books for children and teenagers. Several of these books have won awards for children's and youth literature in South Africa.